little senses

Can I Play Too?

by Samantha Cotterill

Dial Books for Young Readers

For Dr. Daly

Dial Books for Young Readers
An imprint of Penguin Random House LLC, New York

Copyright © 2020 by Samantha Cotterill

Visit us online at penguinrandomhouse.com

Library of Congress Cataloging-in-Publication Data
Names: Cotterill, Samantha, author.
Title: Can I play too? / Samantha Cotterill.
Description: New York : Dial Books for Young Readers, [2020] | Series: Little senses | Audience: Ages 3–7. | Audience: Grades K–1.
Summary: "A young boy building a train track with his friend is headed for trouble until a teacher steps in and helps him learn social cues of anger and happiness"—Provided by publisher.
Identifiers: LCCN 2019038787 (print) | LCCN 2019038788 (ebook) | ISBN 9780525553465 (hardcover) | ISBN 9781984815972 (kindle edition) | ISBN 9781984815965 (ebook)
Subjects: CYAC: Emotions—Fiction. | Cooperativeness—Fiction.
Classification: LCC PZ7.1.C6749 Can 2020 (print) | LCC PZ7.1.C6749 (ebook) | DDC [E]—dc23
LC record available at https://lccn.loc.gov/2019038787
LC ebook record available at https://lccn.loc.gov/2019038788

Printed in China

ISBN 9780525553465

10 9 8 7 6 5 4 3

Design by Mina Chung • Text set in Futura and Cooper Md
This art was created with ink with some pencil on watercolor paper.

Can I play too?

Okay!

Let's build a track!

Sure!

Click!

Clack!

Snap!

This piece goes there.

And that one here.

Not there . . .

I'll fix it!

There!

You found my favorite one!

I know just the spot.

**This is so much fun!
I LOVE trains.**

**Did you know some trains can travel
100 miles per hour through tunnels?**

One time my dad took me
on a real train.

Ooh!

This piece goes . . .

Tug tug...

Pull pull...

Heave ho!

You ruined
the track!

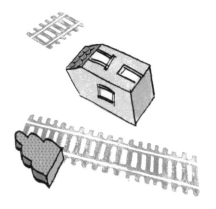

Did you know that trains depend
on traffic lights to run smoothly?

Green says "okay to go!"

Yellow warns
"better go slow . . ."

Red means
"stop,"
but—oh, no!

What do you think
will happen next?

CRASH!

Friends have traffic signals too.

And once you learn them,
you'll know just what to do!

Your friend smiled so big when
you asked him to play . . .

Whoot woo!
I'm proud of you!

His smile turned to a frown when
he wanted a turn . . .

. . . and then he became angry
when he felt unheard.

Try a do-over and see
what can happen.

Want to play again?

Ooh!

What's wrong?

I had that . . .

I'm sorry. **Thanks.**

Click!

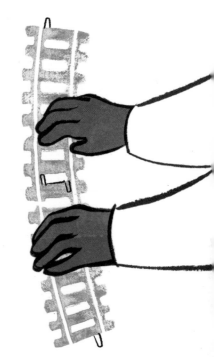

Clack!

Snap!

Chugga,
chugga...
Chugga,
chugga...

Whoot!
Woo!